# The Parade

JANETTA OTTER-BARRY BOOKS

*The Parade* copyright © Frances Lincoln Limited 2010
Text copyright © KP Kojo 2010
Illustrations copyright © Karen Lilje 2010

First published in Great Britain in 2010 by
Frances Lincoln Children's Books, 4 Torriano Mews,
Torriano Avenue, London NW5 2RZ

www.franceslincoln.com

A catalogue record for this book is available from the British Library

ISBN-978-1-84780-012-1

Set in Charis SIL

Printed in Croydon, Surrey, UK by CPI Bookmarque Ltd. in July 2010

1 3 5 7 9 8 6 4 2

# The Parade

## A Stampede of Stories about Ananse, the Trickster Spider

## KP Kojo

### Illustrated by Karen Lilje

**F**

FRANCES LINCOLN
CHILDREN'S BOOKS

*For Omara Okailey, Jerome Ayitey, Cameron,*
*Jean Ayikailey and Sarah Marie*

# Contents

# introduction

Ananse has been in existence since the early Ashanti kingdom, when tales about the spider trickster were told as a means of passing on customs, knowledge and etiquette. The stories were a source of great entertainment for children, and proverbs from the tales became part of everyday speech. So it's not surprising that Ananse survived the transatlantic slave trade and surfaced in the Caribbean as Anancy or Brer Nancy, eventually making it into print over there.

Amongst the Akan in Ghana, however, the stories continue to be told orally. When my family moved to Cape Coast, Ghana, in 1979, Ananse immediately became a daily part of my life. We stayed with friends of my father's in a communal house for three months, and at least once a day someone would stop my brother and me to tell us Ananse stories. It took me a while to get used to the Akan vocabulary, since I only spoke Ga and English at the time, but the telling was so physical and funny that it didn't take long for me to understand. Once my command of Akan improved, my enjoyment of the tales deepened, but there were two questions that always hovered in the background. Where did Ananse's wife come from? And why did Ananse become a trickster?

Those questions were the main triggers for me to write the title story in this collection, an original Ananse story that draws on the authentic tradition of encapsulating origin myths of animals, pointers for good behaviour and examples of Ananse's inventive thinking. I also wanted to reproduce the fun and urgency of the oral storytelling ~ the vibrant atmosphere that is created when an aunt or uncle is telling the stories and stops to emphasise the funny moments.

The final element in *The Parade* is the fusion of Ghanaian languages in the naming of the animals. I have used Twi, Ga, Ewe, Hausa and Dagbani names, sometimes combinations of two, to emphasise that Ananse tales have become defining stories for most of Ghana – not just the Ashanti – an indicator of how powerful and compelling they are.

I hope that you enjoy reading and sharing them as much as I enjoyed growing up with them.

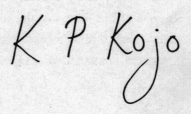

# The Parade

Once upon a long time ago, in the forest of Aboakrom, there lived a spider called Ananse. He was a farmer, and he lived at the edge of a cliff called Fom, beside a deep lake.

Ananse always liked to tell a good tale and all the animals knew him as a fun-loving joker. They preferred him to his friend Adanko the rabbit, who was a known trickster.

The head cat, Muzuru, who was also the wisest animal and the master of the Aboakrom school, always said, "Ananse is an outstanding student and a very sociable fellow."

That was all very well, but Ananse had grown up now and he was lonely. He wanted a wife so that he would have someone to talk to. Someone to swim in the lake with.

Ananse's big secret was that he was in love with the girl that Ketebo the leopard was courting. A girl called Aso Yaa, who had the most beautiful voice in all of Aboakrom.

☼ ☼ ☼

One day, while walking home from his farm, Ananse told his secret to Adanko the rabbit.

Adanko pricked his ears and laughed. "Oh, poor Ananse! You mean you want the same girl that the leopard wants? Ha ha ha ha!" Adanko rolled on his back and waved his paws in the air.

Ananse was very upset. "Adanko," he said. "Why are you laughing? I thought you were

my friend." He pointed four of his eight legs at Adanko. "I'll show you!" he cried. Then he stormed off home alone.

Now, the reason why Ketebo the leopard still hadn't married Aso Yaa was her father, Opanyin. He was a cunning old man, and his one wish was to see all the animals of Aboakrom in a parade before he died. He promised to give his daughter's hand to anyone who could make this happen.

Many suitors had failed, but Ketebo had nearly succeeded. He had bullied most of the animals into a parade, but because he couldn't bully Fangbini the tiger and Gyata the lion, he had failed. So, as you can see, bullying doesn't really get you anywhere.

As Ananse walked home, he couldn't stop thinking about how his friend Adanko the trickster had laughed at him. So he came up with a plan – he would trick the trickster. He was going to show Adanko and make Aso Yaa his wife. As he got closer to home his smile got wider and WIDER and he skipped over to the cliff, clicking his fingers and toes.

When Ananse got home, he found an old green shirt in his bedroom and he tore it to make a flag. Then he climbed a young vine tree to get a rope to tie to the flag. After all that, Ananse was very tired so he went to sleep.

❂ ❂ ❂

The next morning, before the sun had even washed its face, Ananse ran to the thickest cluster of trees in Aboakrom forest and called for Akoo the parrot.

"Akoo! Akoo!"

Akoo almost fell off her perch on the branch. "What? What?" She opened her eyes and saw the spider below her. "Oh, Ananse! What are you doing up at this early hour?"

"I need your help, Akoo."

Akoo flapped her wings and came down to Ananse. "Listen," she said in a stern voice. "You can't come and wake me up this early in the morning and expect me to help you. What is in it for me?"

"Akoo, do you remember when Adanko the rabbit made you sick by dipping your berries in pepper?" Ananse asked.

Akoo frowned until her yellow face became brighter than her red tail feathers. "Oh, that rabbit! I will teach him a lesson one day!"

13

"Well!" Ananse smiled and took out the flag he had made the night before. "If you just carry this flag and follow Adanko, he will be taught a lesson before night comes. Just fly to the anthill beside the big mango tree and wait. That's where Adanko usually hides."

"With pleasure." Akoo took the flag from Ananse and went to wash her face.

Ananse skipped off to see Kitre the lizard. "Has Adanko ever tricked you?" he asked.

"Yes." The lizard nodded.

Ananse whispered into Kitre's ear and the lizard nodded some more.

Next, Ananse went to Dorina Kɛsiɛ the hippopotamus.

"Has Adanko the rabbit ever tricked you?"

Dorina Kɛsiɛ's nostrils widened with rage. "Of course he has tricked me. Who hasn't he tricked?"

So Ananse climbed up the hippo's head and whispered into her ear.

The hippo smiled and showed her great big gums.

Next, Ananse went to Rago the goat, then Pongo the horse, then Muzuru the cat, then Shuo the elephant, then Dun the monkey, then Ketebo the leopard, then Fangbini the tiger, then Avu the dog, then Nufowo the snake....

o o o

By the time the sun opened its mouth to yawn *good morning*, Ananse had spoken to all the animals of Aboakrom. All except Adanko the rabbit.

Ananse was tired from all his running around, so he rested for a minute beneath the big baobab tree near the river Nsu. Then he crossed the bridge and went home to bathe in the lake. He put on his best clothes and a wide hat, and then he went to Opanyin's house with a pot of fresh, sweet palm wine.

In the yard of Opanyin's house, Aso Yaa was sweeping dried leaves into a heap, and Opanyin was sitting in a chair cleaning his teeth with a neem stick.

Ananse raised his hat and greeted Aso Yaa. "Beautiful lady, I greet you."

Aso Yaa smiled but kept sweeping.

Ananse walked over to her father and put

the pot of palm wine down. He took off his hat and said, "Wise Opanyin, I greet you."

Opanyin nodded and smiled. "Good morning to you, Ananse. To what do I owe this morning visit?"

Ananse bowed. "Opanyin, I have come with wine to ask for your daughter's hand in marriage."

Opanyin laughed. "You are a brave young man to take on Ketebo, but you know what I have asked for. I am old and I will die soon. The only thing I want is to see a parade of all the animals of Aboakrom before I die. If you give me that, my daughter is yours."

"Thank you, Opanyin." Ananse bowed again. "If I could humbly ask you to come and sit by the bridge that leads to my house and drink some palm wine with me, your wish will be granted by sundown."

So Ananse carried three chairs to the right bank of the river Nsu and sat there drinking palm wine with Opanyin and Aso Yaa.

Meanwhile, Adanko was in his hiding place by the anthill eating kontomire. He didn't know Akoo the parrot was sitting above the anthill with a green flag tied to her waist. He didn't know that Ananse had told all the animals of Aboakrom to look for a green flag if they wanted to see where Adanko hid during the day.

So Adanko the rabbit was in his hiding place when the earth began to shake.

'Oh, no,' he thought, 'an earthquake.' He peeked out of his front door and lo and behold... it was a stampede of animals. Heading straight...

TO HIS HIDING PLACE!

Oh, no! Adanko knew that he had played tricks on all the animals, so he had to run. He closed the front door of his hiding place and bolted it. Then he slipped out of the back door and took off faster than lightning.

Akoo the parrot heard a noise behind her and turned to see Adanko the rabbit running. She took off with a squawk and followed him. The green flag that Ananse had made fluttered behind her and ALL the other animals followed.

Now, because Ananse and Adanko used to be good friends, Ananse knew that whenever Adanko was in trouble he ran to the cliff to ask

Ananse for help. The thing is, to get to where Ananse lived, you had to cross the river Nsu. And the only way to cross the river Nsu was by the bridge where Ananse was sitting with Opanyin and Aso Yaa. So the three of them sat there, drinking palm wine.

Before long, they heard a quick rustling in the long grass and, in the blink of an eye, Adanko the rabbit darted across the bridge. He was followed closely by Akoo, flapping her wings wildly, and then all the other animals came trooping past on the bridge.

Pongo the horse galloped past...

Nufowo the snake slithered by...

Dorina Kɛsiɛ the hippo thundered along...

Tsina the cow streaked through....

Gyata the lion pranced past....

Dun the monkey swung by...

Avu the dog charged through...

Kada the crocodile zigzagged across...
Aburuburu the pigeon flew along...
Kitre the lizard skittered past...
Shuo the elephant trumpeted by...
Muzuru the cat slunk across...
Kpoto the pig waddled along....

It was the longest parade of animals ever – you could see them from the bridge all the way to the edge of Aboakrom, where the sun was beginning to set.

Ananse, Opanyin and Aso Yaa clapped with glee, while poor Adanko ran to the edge of the cliff - but couldn't find Ananse to help him.

When Adanko realised that Ananse wasn't at the edge of the cliff to help him, he began to dig a hole in the ground to hide in. He dug so quickly that by the time the animals made it to the edge, Adanko had vanished.

Most of the animals managed to stop, but Dorina Kɛsiɛ the hippo and Shuo the elephant were too heavy and couldn't stop. They went over the edge of the cliff and fell, SPLASH, into the middle of the lake. Shuo managed to get out by sucking the water in front of him and spraying it behind him with his long nose, but Dorina Kɛsiɛ the hippo liked the cool water, and stayed in it. She still lives there now.

☼ ☼ ☼

This is how Ananse became known as a trickster and won Aso Yaa's hand in marriage. He became enemies with Adanko the rabbit, who now lives in a hole in the ground. Of course, now you also know why hippos live in water.

# The Pot of Stories

In faraway Aboakrom, where Ananse the spider lived, night came early, swooping down like a black crow at exactly six o'clock. Never a minute earlier, never a minute later. It was as though the sun suddenly hid its head under a bush – everything turned completely black, except for a faraway yellow light, round and pale. It shone from the home of the chief of the entire forest, Nana Oppong, lord of the trees as far as the eye could see.

Nana Oppong's home was a palace in the sky. Here he stayed up after nightfall making up stories, which he hid in a big, brown, clay pot.

Now Nana Oppong was a very grumpy man and he did not like to be disturbed when he was working. He made a law that forbade anyone in the forest to move or speak after night came. He kept all his stories to himself and never shared them. So the forest was as quiet as a whisper at night, and all the animals fell asleep because they were bored.

After a while, Ayelo the owl, who liked to fly around at night, got very upset and decided to go and complain to Nana Oppong. But because Nana Oppong was a very, very grumpy man, Ayelo the owl was scared – too scared to go alone. So he decided to ask Ananse to go with him.

Ananse had shown himself to be very wise in winning his wife Aso Yaa's hand in marriage. Since that time, many of the animals had made trips to the edge of the cliff, Fom, where he lived, to consult him about their problems.

When Ananse heard Ayelo the owl's problem, he got angry himself because he had never had the chance to tell his young son Ntikuma any stories when he was growing up.

He nodded vigorously, peering at the owl and tapping three of his feet. Then he said, "Let's go. Everyone should be able to speak when they want to."

With that, Ananse jumped on to Ayelo's back and Ayelo took off. She spread her wings wide, flapped them twice and glided off to Nana Oppong's palace.

☼ ☼ ☼

The first morning, Nana Oppong refused to see them because it was daytime, and that was when he rested. He stayed in bed and got his assistants to lock all his doors and windows.

So the next morning, Ananse and Ayelo returned with sticks and started singing and playing music on Nana Oppong's windows.

Nana Oppong ignored them, but he couldn't sleep, so that night he was unable to write any stories. He was very cross.

The third morning, when Ayelo and Ananse arrived, Nana Oppong flung his front door open and yelled, "What do you want?"

Ayelo the owl stuttered, "To, to, to, to… be allowed to fly at night."

"To be able to tell stories to our children," Ananse added.

Nana Oppong laughed when he heard the word stories. "Do you even know any stories?" he asked.

"No," said Ananse, "but if you let us move while we sleep, we will be able to dream - and when we dream, we will be able to make up stories."

Now, of course, Nana Oppong didn't want anyone else to have stories, because HIS stories would no longer be special. But he didn't want Ananse and Ayelo to keep disturbing his sleep, so he thought of a cunning plan to get rid of them.

He rubbed his big round belly and licked his lips. "OK," he said, pointing at Ananse. "I will give you a task. If you fail, everyone will have to stay quiet and still for longer every day.

If you succeed, I will give you my pot of stories and everyone can do what they like."

Ananse and Ayelo started shaking, because they knew Nana Oppong could be very mean.

Then Nana Oppong said, "If you're scared, you can just go home, and all of Aboakrom will have to continue to follow my rules."

Ananse looked at Ayelo, who was so miserable that his huge eyes looked like glasses of water. And he thought about his son, going to sleep every day with no stories. "I'll do the task," he said.

"Well," said Nana Oppong, clapping his hands with glee, "it's simple. I want you to bring me a live python, a live lion and a swarm of honey bees. You have seven days."

Ananse and Ayelo left Nana Oppong's palace in silence, very nervous. Ayelo flew so low in the trees that Auako the hawk stopped him.

"Ayelo," the hawk asked, "have you forgotten how to fly? Why are you so low?"

Ayelo sighed, and told Auako about the task that Nana Oppong had given. "I think I've made things worse for everyone," the owl hooted.

But Ananse held up a foot. "Let us not panic yet. I will go home and sleep on the problem. I'm sure there is a solution."

☼ ☼ ☼

The next morning Ananse woke up his wife Aso Yaa, and his son Ntikuma, with a big smile on his face. "I have a plan to catch the python and the lion," he said, "but I will need your help."

"We will do anything you need," said Aso Yaa and Ntikuma.

"OK." Ananse jumped from his seat. "Aso Yaa, could you please weave me two very strong ropes, a basket and the strongest sack ever woven?"

"Of course, my dear." And off went Aso Yaa, towards the raffia trees in the middle of the forest.

"Ntikuma." Ananse turned to his son. "You will be coming with me. Get me the sturdiest walking stick you can find, and let's go."

Soon, Ananse and Ntikuma were close to the edge of the forest where the python lived. Ananse clutched the walking stick like an old man, dragging his feet behind him.

He argued with Ntikuma in a very loud voice. "Don't bring my stick into this," he screamed. "I said, don't bring my stick into this. My stick is longer than any snake."

Ntikuma shook his head, knowing – of course – that they were close enough for the python to hear them. "But this is not just any snake. It's a python – a royal python."

"I don't care if your python is royal or common. It is still puny, and shorter than my stick."

When the python heard this, she was furious and could barely keep still. She slid out from her hiding place beneath some dead leaves and asked, "What is the problem here?"

Ananse grunted and ignored her, rubbing his back as though it hurt.

Ntikuma walked up to the python and whispered, "My grandfather thinks you are puny and that his walking stick is bigger than you. I've told him you are bigger, but he doesn't believe me."

"Of course I'm bigger than his stick."

"I don't believe you," Ananse shouted.

"I am," said the python.

"You're not," said Ananse.

"She is," said Ntikuma.

"Then prove it." Ananse stamped four feet on the ground.

Ntikuma turned to the python. "Will you help me? All you have to do is lie beside the stick."

"Fine," spat the python.

"I'm not giving you my stick," Ananse frowned.

"Oh, please," said Ntikuma. "Let's settle this once and for all."

Ananse shook his head.

"Please." Both Ntikuma and the python begged.

Ananse threw his stick to Ntikuma.

As soon as the python lay beside the stick, Ananse and Ntikuma tied her to it with the rope that Aso Yaa had woven. They carried the python home and put her in the basket.

☼ ☼ ☼

The next day, Ananse and Ntikuma headed to the green clearing in front of the lion's den and started another argument.

"I tell you he's fit, he'll fit," Ananse declared.

Ntikuma stamped on a weed. "No, he's too fat, he'll never fit."

"No, he's fit, he'll fit."

"Fat. Won't fit."

"Fit."

"Fat."

They went on like this, getting louder and louder until the lion, who was sleeping, woke up with a roar and emerged from his den.

"What is this racket about? I am trying to sleep."

Ananse and Ntikuma stood very still and didn't speak. They had a plan, but they were quite afraid of the huge lion.

"Well?" growled the lion. "Are you going to tell me?"

"Erm," Ananse stuttered, holding out the sack that Aso Yaa had woven. "My, my, my... my son is very disrespectful. Sorry. He thinks you're too fat to fit in this sack."

The lion frowned. "I'm fat?"

"He said it." Ananse pointed at Ntikuma. "It's the young people these days. They have no respect."

"I'm FAT?" The lion stared at Ntikuma, who nodded feebly. "Well, watch this, young man," he said - and jumped nimbly into the sack.

Of course, straightaway Ananse and Ntikuma tied him in the sack and dragged him home, laughing all the way.

❂ ❂ ❂

The next two days Ananse went walking alone in the forest, trying to think of ways in which he could catch a swarm of bees. He returned home upset and hungry, with no ideas at all. He sent Ntikuma to tell Ayelo the owl that he had failed the task.

At dinner Ananse ate his boiled groundnuts in silence and stared at the floor. He had given up.

Suddenly, Aso Yaa spoke. "I have an idea for you."

Ananse sighed. "Let's hear it."

"Well, when I was draining your groundnuts through the sieve, the water looked a lot like rain. And we all know bees don't like water."

"Ah!" Ananse and Ntikuma clapped loudly.

They collected a few things from the kitchen, hugged Aso Yaa and set off towards the bees' tree in a hurry.

The bees lived on the lower branches of a huge tree that usually protected them from rain. When our friends Ananse and Ntikuma arrived at the tree, Ntikuma climbed on to the branch just above the bees' hive, and Ananse passed him a jug of water and Aso Yaa's sieve. Then Ananse stood ready with an open glass jar and winked at Ntikuma.

Ntikuma poured water through the sieve on to the bees' hive.

In seconds the bees emerged, buzzing.

"Oh no, it's a storm. We're going to drown."

"Oh no, somebody help!"

Ananse, naturally, was waiting to do just that. "Bees," he cried, "if you get into this glass jar the rain can't touch you. You will be safe."

And because they hated water so much, the bees swarmed into the jar without asking any questions.

Ananse quickly shut the jar and headed to Ayelo's house with Ntikuma.

Ayelo the owl widened his huge eyes when Ananse showed him the jar of live bees. "But…" He shook his head.

"Everything is fine now," said Ananse. "I just need you to ask Auako the hawk to help us carry the snake and the lion to Nana Oppong's."

Ayelo's eyes opened even wider. "You have them all?"

"Yes," Ntikuma shrieked, very proud of his father.

☼ ○ ○ ○

Now, if you think Ayelo was surprised, imagine
how stunned Nana Oppong was when he opened
the door to his palace to be presented with a
live python, a live lion and a swarm of bees.
Ananse and Ayelo had completed his impossible
task three days early!

Nana Oppong was a sore loser. He refused to hand over his pot of stories to Ayelo and Ananse. In a wild rage he picked up the pot and flung it on the floor. It shattered with a loud BANG, breaking all Nana Oppong's windows.

The stories scattered all over the place. Some got stuck in corners, some flapped in the wind and got carried far away. Some bits flew through the windows and got stuck in people's hair, some flew as far as the lake by Ananse's house, where the hippo Dorina Kɛsiɛ was resting. Others scattered far, far beyond.

Before long, everyone would have a story in their house. By completing the task, Ananse also made it possible for everyone to toss and turn and dream in their sleep.

☼ ☼ ☼

I bet you're wondering about the python, the lion and the bees. Well, Ananse let them go, of course, but I'm sure you understand now why snakes don't like to lie in a straight line, and why bees live in holes rather than out in the open. As for the lion, he's still quite upset. Somewhere out there you can hear him roaring.

# The Return
# of Leopard

Now, do you remember that a leopard used to live in Aboakrom? His name was Ketebo and he was the one Ananse outwitted to win the hand of his wife, Aso Yaa, in marriage.

Well, Ketebo never forgot Aso Yaa. He was a sore loser and he was still besotted with her.

After hiding away for many years in shame, he returned to Aboakrom and started to follow Aso Yaa around. Every time she went to the market Ketebo would slink after her, lying in wait for her and trying to sing to her. When she went to the well to fetch water in the morning, there he was again, his coat gleaming, his sharp teeth bared as he smiled. Aso Yaa felt very scared and told Ananse what Ketebo was doing.

Ananse was working very hard on his farm before the rainy season so he asked his son, Ntikuma, to go with his mother to the well and to the market. Of course, that was not enough to stop the stubborn Ketebo. He chased Ntikuma away – not once, not twice, not even thrice, but four times.

The fourth time he growled, "You, son of a spider, if I ever see you again, I will beat you up. And if I see you another time after that, I will rip you to tiny pieces."

When Ntikuma told Ananse what had happened, he was very angry. He stamped all eight of his feet. "He picked on you? My son? A child?"

Ananse threw down his hoe instantly and set off to the lake near his house to wash the mud off his feet. Then he called all the animals to witness his challenge to Ketebo.

"Aso Yaa is my wife, fair and square," he told Ketebo. "I beat you at one challenge and I will beat you again. Let Aso Yaa's father, Opanyin, pick another task. If I beat you, you must hide from her for ever."

"That's fine with me." Ketebo smiled, showing his huge muscles. "And if I win, I will kill your son and take Aso Yaa with me."

"I didn't say that," Ananse said.

Ketebo laughed. "But you said you would beat me, so why does it matter what I ask?"

Ananse realised that he was trapped, so he turned to Opanyin to wait for the challenge.

Now, Opanyin was one of the most successful farmers in Aboakrom and he owned a large tract of land that stretched for acres and acres. But there was one portion of his land that he had never been able to farm, because it was overgrown with stinging nettles. As wise as ever, he saw this as an opportunity to clear his land.

"My task is this," said Opanyin, raising his arm. "You must each clear a section of my land in the part where the stinging nettles grow. You must clear it without scratching any part of your body. If you scratch, you lose."

Opanyin handed a cutlass each to Ananse and Ketebo and everyone in Aboakrom followed as the wise old man led the two rivals to the land they were to clear. Everyone. It was such a huge crowd that you couldn't count them, but you could just about make out:

Pongo the horse, nodding along…

Nufowo the snake, slithering between legs...

Tsina the cow, giggling with Avu the dog....

All of them in coats of different colours.

It looked like a carnival.

When they got to the stinging nettles, Opanyin walked to a section between two trees and placed a slipper exactly halfway between the two trees. Then he picked up a stone and threw it as far as he could.

"Now," he said, "Ketebo, you clear everything from the right side of the slipper to that tree until you get to the stone. Ananse, you clear the rest."

"Is that all?" Ketebo asked, flexing his muscles again. "I'll be finished before sundown."

Ananse said nothing.

Opanyin clapped his hands. "I haven't finished. Whoever finishes first wins, but if neither of you finishes clearing, my daughter will move back home with me. Remember, if you scratch, you lose."

Everyone was quiet as they waited for Ananse and Ketebo to start clearing.

Ananse sat beneath the tree on his side and crossed his legs. "You start, Ketebo," he said, "I'm in no rush."

All the animals gasped, wondering why Ananse would offer a head start to someone so much stronger than him.

Ketebo frowned. He was sure Ananse was up to something, but he couldn't think what. "You must be mad. I am bigger than you and I am stronger than you. You will never catch up with me."

"Oh, I will catch up with you," Ananse smiled. "I will show you just how strong I am."

"Do you think you're stronger than me?" Ketebo demanded angrily. "I will show you." And with that, Ketebo bared his sharp teeth, flexed his arms and legs, and started clearing.

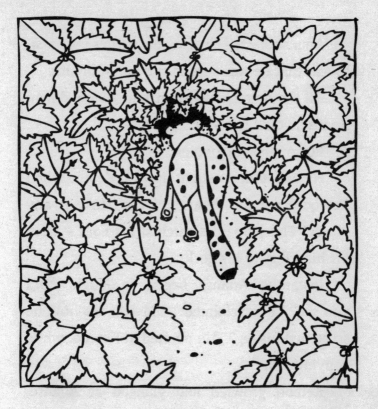

Ananse knew that Ketebo had a fine, thick coat, so it would take a while before the nettles got to his skin and made him itch. He waited until Ketebo had cleared a few yards and had started to pause after each swing of his cutlass – a sure sign that he had begun to itch – before he began.

Ananse started clearing the nettles very fast, so fast that he was sure to run out of breath.

All the animals yelled at him. "Slow down, Ananse, you'll tire yourself out."

But Ananse carried on.

He had almost caught up with Ketebo when Ketebo screamed. "Aargh. I can't take it any more." The leopard scratched his coat – from his hind legs to his neck.

Instantly, Ananse began to laugh. "Did you see?" he exclaimed. "Did you see how he scratched his leg?" He pointed at Ketebo, while copying him.

Ketebo growled and glanced at Ananse, waiting for his rival to scratch himself too, but Ananse kept on clearing the nettles. Ananse had slowed down now and was making steady progress.

In order not to lose face, Ketebo carried on clearing his side of the plot – no way would he let his puny rival finish before he did – but after every three swings of his cutlass he would stop and scratch himself.

And each time Ketebo scratched himself, Ananse would stop, laugh and imitate him.

By sundown, both Ananse and Ketebo had finished, and Ananse had still not scratched himself. Ketebo, on the other hand, had scratched himself so badly that he had sores all over his golden coat.

Everyone in Aboakrom clapped as Ananse embraced Aso Yaa and Ntikuma.

As Ananse walked home with his family, Aso Yaa whispered, "How did you do it?"

Ananse smiled. "Every time I laughed, I was actually screaming. The trick was to give Ketebo a head start. To win by starting last. When he scratched, I scratched, but I made it look like I was laughing at him." Ananse grabbed Aso Yaa's hand and rubbed Ntikuma's head.

○ ○ ○

As for our friend Ketebo the leopard, he slunk off deep into the forest in shame and when his sores healed, they became dark patches on his coat. So, naturally, you won't be surprised to see a leopard with spots, because you know how he got them!

# Hot Beans in a Hat

After Ananse's success against Ketebo the leopard, his fame grew far and wide.

Everywhere Akoo the parrot flew, he chattered about Ananse's quick thinking, and how he had arranged a parade of animals for Opanyin without anyone knowing.

When Ayelo the owl went on his night flights, he cooed to everyone who would listen, that he was able to fly at night because of Ananse's cunning.

And of course, every resident of Aboakrom

had witnessed Ananse's battle with Opanyin's stinging nettles. It had now become common practice to go to Ananse for advice – even his old teacher Muzuru, the cat, had asked him for help in resolving his differences with Avu the dog.

Ananse became quite proud. At home, he expected special treatment. He left rubbish on the floor and demanded that Aso Yaa and Ntikuma clean up after him. He took the best cuts of meat from the cooking pot before anyone else could eat. And he never thanked them. On the streets, he walked with his head held high, raising his hands to receive cheers from passers-by. He didn't ask for anything; he expected everything to be given to him.

Aso Yaa's father, Opanyin, had noticed the change in Ananse, his once-humble son-in-law. When Opanyin's last daughter, Okonirie, had a baby, he saw it as a perfect chance to teach Ananse a lesson.

Opanyin arranged an outdooring feast and invited all his family, including Aso Yaa, Ntikuma and Ananse. He ordered all the food you can imagine – plantain chips, rice and peas, kontomire, pizza, strawberries, fufu and soup, pasta, noodles, mangoes, waache, watermelons, fish and chips, yɛlɛ, carrots, jollof rice... you just had to think of it and it was there.

All the dishes you can imagine, except one – Ananse's favourite.

Hot beans!

When Ananse and his family arrived at the feast, Opanyin welcomed them with a big grin, hugging them all before showing them to their seats. Ananse was very excited, because he knew his mother-in-law, Mama Aba, made the best beans in Aboakrom.

He was wearing his best clothes – a black and brown suit with a high top hat – and was all smiles as he held the new baby and waited for the food to come to the dining room. "What a beautiful little baby," he said, rocking the child in his arms. "Ntikuma was this tiny many years ago; now he eats more than I do."

Opanyin laughed. "Don't worry about Ntikuma's appetite today. We have plenty of food for everyone."

"I'm looking forward to the food," Ananse smiled.

And so the food began to arrive.

Ananse took a seat opposite Opanyin and watched. His mouth watered as plates of plantain chips, rice and peas, kontomire, pizza, strawberries, fufu and soup, pasta, noodles, mangoes, waache, watermelons, fish and chips, yɛlɛ, carrots and jollof rice piled up on the huge table. His eyes darted back and forth, taking it all in, wondering when the hot beans would arrive.

When everyone was seated and had begun to eat, he realised that there were no hot beans. Ananse was furious.

What was Opanyin playing at? Everyone knew that he, Ananse, the wise one, liked hot beans. What was the point of inviting him to a party with no hot beans? Ananse took a small serving of jollof rice and glared at Opanyin.

The thing is, there WERE hot beans in the house. Opanyin had simply asked the cooks not to bring the beans to the table, to test Ananse, to see if his pride would stop him from using his quick wits wisely.

So the beans remained on the stove, simmering away in Mama Aba's special spice mix and the reddest palm oil ever. It smelled delicious – and, after a while, the smell began to drift through the house.

Ananse, who was chewing on a mouthful of jollof rice with a glum look on his face, lifted his head and sniffed. 'Ah,' he thought, 'there is a pot of hot beans SOMEWHERE in this house and they are trying to hide it from me.'

Ananse looked around the big table. His wife, Aso Yaa, was playing with the new baby, Opanyin was talking to Okonorie, Ntikuma was trying to stuff a huge piece of akrantiɛ meat into his mouth – everyone was having a great time.

Ananse had been sulking since the food arrived, but no one had noticed. "They don't care about me," he muttered to himself. He sniffed the air again, then he stood up. "Excuse me," he said, "I have to go to the toilet. I think I have an upset stomach."

As soon as Ananse left the dining room, he rushed to the back yard where Mama Aba did her cooking. There were many pots there, so it was hard to find the one containing hot beans. But Ananse sniffed and sniffed and sniffed until – finally – he found the pot with the beans.

He rubbed his belly, lifting the lid off the pot, then dipped a finger in the pot and licked it.

The beans were deeee-li-cious! They smelled of peppers and bay leaves and were submerged in rich palm oil the colour of an intense red sunset. Ananse couldn't help himself. Although the beans were piping hot, he plunged three of his hands into the pot and stuffed some beans into his mouth.

He screamed as the beans burned his tongue, then tried to muffle the sound with his palms so that no one would hear him from the dining room. The beans were so tasty that Ananse licked his fingers six times before he wiped his face and returned to the feast.

"Ananse," Opanyin cried as Ananse walked back in. "Are you OK? We heard you screaming."

"Oh, that?" Ananse shifted from foot to foot as though he was dancing on nails. "It was from the pain of my stomach ache. It's really quite bad."

And with that he sat down, happy that he

had deceived everyone and tasted the best hot beans in the world – alone.

The whole family went back to having fun at the feast, and Ananse went back to his plate of jollof rice. He took a morsel of it, but the rice didn't taste good any more. He tried some okro stew with banku, but that didn't taste good either. He tried another dish.

In fact he tried everything at the feast: plantain chips, rice and peas, kontomire, pizza, strawberries, fufu and soup, pasta, noodles, mangoes, waache, watermelons, fish and chips, yɛlɛ, carrots….

Any food you can think of, Ananse tried, but nothing could take his mind off the delicious hot beans. He could still smell them and all he could think about was how red the palm oil was and how good Mama Aba's spice mix tasted with the beans.

He sniffed the air and stood up. "Excuse me again," he said.

"What's wrong now?" asked his wife, Aso Yaa.

"My stomach," moaned Ananse. "I think it's diarrhoea."

"Oh, you poor spider. Should I come with you?" said Aso Yaa.

Ananse shook his head. "No, no, no... I'll be just fine." He crept out of the dining room, holding his belly.

By now, Opanyin had grown suspicious and he decided to ask Ananse some questions when he returned to the table.

Of course Ananse didn't know this and, as soon as he closed the door to the dining room behind him, he ran to the back yard in glee. When he got to the pot of hot beans, he plunged three hands in – as before – and filled his mouth with the hot, sweet and spicy beans. He screamed again, licked his fingers, wiped his face and turned to go back to the feast. But, right outside the door of the dining room, he had a brilliant idea and ran back to the pot of hot beans.

Ananse took off his hat and placed it beside the pot of hot beans. He filled the hat with the spiced beans and palm oil sauce and wore the hat.

The beans were so hot that when he got back to the feast Ananse could barely stand.

He wanted to get Aso Yaa and Ntikuma to leave with him right away, but before he could speak, Opanyin addressed him.

"Ananse, is something wrong with the food we have served?"

"Oh, no, no, no." Ananse opened his eyes wide, trying not to scream. "It must be something I ate earlier." He turned to Aso Yaa and Ntikuma. "Let's go. In my condition, it's probably better that we go home."

"But I've just started playing with the baby," Aso Yaa said.

"We really should go," Ananse insisted, closing one eye in pain.

Opanyin went up to Ananse and felt his neck. "Your temperature seems fine, Ananse. Maybe you should wait. If you really have diarrhoea you'll need to go to the toilet again very soon."

"But, but…" Ananse struggled to find something to say in response, but he was trapped by his own lie.

Everyone was looking at him – all the grown-ups and children, even the new baby. There was no way out.

With a loud cry, Ananse threw his hat off, spilling the hot beans across the room. You can imagine the look of shock on everyone's faces. Some of them even had to duck under the table to avoid being covered in hot beans.

Opanyin shook his head and said, "Ananse, if you wanted hot beans, why didn't you just ask?"

"I... I... I..." Ananse realised that he had been silly and, before he could answer, all the children started laughing and pointing at his head.

You see, with all the heat from the spicy beans, Ananse's hair had burnt off, leaving him with a head as smooth as a seaside pebble.

Ananse slowly raised a hand to his head and when he realised what had happened he hid beneath the table.

So, if you have ever wondered why spiders hide in dark places when there are a lot of people around, now you know. And if anyone asks why spiders are bald, you can tell them about Ananse's pride at the outdooring feast.

# The Sticky Scuffle

Not long after the day of the feast came days of hunger, the time of the great drought. Food was scarce and it was not uncommon to see Pongo the horse fighting with his cousin Damusa the donkey over the same dry patch of grass, or to see Akoo the parrot and Richia the pigeon squabbling over a stray kernel of maize.

It hadn't rained for months and months in Aboakrom. Even the lake beside Ananse's house at Fom, where Dorina Kɛsiɛ the hippo liked to relax, was almost dry.

None of the farmers had enough water to raise their crops. Ananse's farm had only produced one basket of black-eyed beans, and even Opanyin's large farm – including the section with nettles that Ananse and Ketebo the leopard had cleared – had only produced twenty ears of maize, two baskets of broad beans, a few onions and three quarter-full baskets of tomatoes.

There was not enough to feed everyone in Aboakrom.

ö ö ö

It was Muzuru, the head cat, who had the idea. Why didn't they go to Nana Oppong and ask him for some land near Nsupa, the stream that never dries? The land there was still fertile and if they worked together on it they could make sure everyone in Aboakrom had food to eat.

Everyone thought this was a brilliant idea and congratulated Muzuru on his wisdom in a time of need. Ananse, however, felt a little jealous because he had become used to being called the wisest person in Aboakrom. He tried hard to think of better ideas than Muzuru's but he couldn't think of any, so he had to go along with everyone else.

Soon the communal farm was thriving. Everyone worked in turns on different days of the week. For example, Pongo the horse and his cousin Damusa the donkey were part of the group that worked on Tuesdays. Tsina the cow and Kada the crocodile worked on Thursdays. Gyata the lion, Rago the goat and Nufowo the snake worked on Saturdays. Everyone worked – except Ananse.

Ananse's excuse was that he had a very serious backache. Every time Ntikuma and Aso Yaa got ready to go to the farm on Wednesdays, Ananse would start moaning and writhing in his bed. Aso Yaa had tried every kind of ointment possible to help heal the

backache but nothing seemed to work.

Of course, the backache seemed to get better later in the week and Ananse tried to work on his own farm, hoping to show everyone that he could make crops grow with very little water.

After many weeks, Ananse's farm had yielded nothing, but the communal farm continued to thrive. Aso Yaa and Ntikuma went to the farm every Saturday with the rest of the residents of Aboakrom to collect their share of yams, beans, groundnuts, pepper, tomatoes, onions, corn, palm nuts, plantain, cassava and fruits. They shared their food with Ananse, but because he didn't work on the communal farm no food could be collected for him. So he never had enough to eat, and he began to get thin.

Curiously, Ananse began to limp out of the house for a couple of hours every night, and soon after that, he stopped losing weight – he got plump. Since he wasn't getting much to eat Aso Yaa was surprised, but Ananse said that it was because he spent more time in bed with backache.

"And where have you been going at night?" Aso Yaa asked.

"I've been getting herbs for my backache," Ananse said. "I think it's working. Look." He took a few steps without limping.

"Well," said Aso Yaa, "that means you'll soon be able to join us on the farm."

Ananse shook his head. "I don't think so. The pain is still too much."

Aso Yaa sighed and went outside to find Ntikuma.

☼ ☼ ☼

Then, one morning, Muzuru – the head cat – stopped by Ananse's house.

"*Agoo*," Muzuru called. "Greetings."

Aso Yaa opened the door. "Oh, Muzuru, come in. Ananse's here." She took Muzuru to the sitting room, where Ananse and Ntikuma were playing draughts.

"Greetings, Muzuru," said Ananse. "Is something wrong?"

Muzuru frowned. "Someone is stealing from our farm. I've come to ask for your help."

"Very odd," said Ananse. "What are they stealing?"

"Mainly fruits, and beans and yams. We have tried everything but they keep escaping. Can you help us catch them?"

Ananse was very happy to be asked to help solve a problem. Since his shame at Opanyin's feast his reputation had suffered and he was glad the animals of Aboakrom had come to realise that he was still the wisest of them all.

But in this case, he couldn't help. He just couldn't.

Ananse looked at Ntikuma and had a great idea. "Muzuru, I am very busy with some trials on my farm, but I'm sure my son Ntikuma can help you. He has done a lot of work with me before."

"Are you sure you can't help yourself?" Muzuru asked.

"I'm sorry, I just can't," said Ananse.

So Muzuru left Ananse's house with Ntikuma, and they went to the communal farm to devise a plan to catch the thief.

When Ntikuma returned home, Ananse asked him what plan he had given Muzuru to catch the thief. But Ntikuma wouldn't tell him.

74

"The thief is from Aboakrom so I can't tell anyone the plan – it could be anyone," said Ntikuma. "I can tell you that the trap has to do with pride."

"Oh," yelled Ananse, "so now you are smarter than your father, are you? Fine, don't tell me. I will show you." He stormed off into the night.

o o o

When the thief arrived at the communal farm that night, he went first for some ripe mangoes and ate them as he walked to the watermelon patch. At the watermelon patch, he split open a juicy melon and scooped the flesh out with three of his hands. It was deee-li-cious!

The thief got up and started to walk towards the yam vines, but just then he spotted another man beside the bean stalks.

He ran to the man. "Hey, what are you

doing here?" he yelled. "Don't you know you are trespassing?"

The man didn't respond.

"Heh, I'm talking to you! You have been caught red-handed."

The man didn't move.

Because it was dark the thief couldn't see the man's face, but he was sure the man was laughing at him.

"Hey, you fool," said the thief, "don't think you can trespass on my patch and laugh at me. I will slap you."

Still the man didn't move. He didn't make a sound.

The thief raised his right hand. "You think I'm joking, don't you? Well, here's a good slap for you."

He swung his hand at the man's cheek – SLAP!

The man didn't flinch and – even worse – the thief's hand got stuck to the man's cheek!

You see, the man was really a gum statue made by Ntikuma to trap the thief. It couldn't move, it couldn't talk – all it could do was be sticky.

Of course the thief didn't know this, so he lost his temper. "Heh," he said to the gum statue, "you had better let go of my hand or I'll have to teach you a lesson. You hear me? I will slap you!" He swung another hand at the gum statue's cheek – SLAP!

And that hand got stuck too.

Now the thief got really, really angry. "Very funny. I have more hands than the average person so don't think I'm done with you." He swung one hand and then another - SLAP! SLAP!

And guess what? They got stuck too!

"Oh," said the thief, "I will show you the power of my legs now. You may be able to hold on to my hands, but my kicks will cripple you. Try this!" He lifted one leg high and struck the gum statue just below the knee – KICK!

And his foot got stuck.

Another KICK!

Stuck.

KICK!

Stuck.

KICK!

Stuck.

Now the thief had no more limbs to use. He had struck the gum statue eight times and each time he had become more and more trapped. He could barely move now, but he was still angry.

"Aha," he boasted, "maybe you haven't heard how strong my head is. Take this!" He butted the gum statue with his bald head – THUMP!

Of course, his head got stuck as well and I'm sure by now you've guessed who the thief was. It was Ananse, the spider – eight limbs and a bald head.

Soon it was morning and, as the sun began

to rise, stretching its arms to touch every corner of the forest, all the residents of Aboakrom gathered with Muzuru and Ntikuma to find out who the thief was. Imagine Muzuru's surprise to find that it was his former student, Ananse, who had been stealing from the communal farm all along!

Ananse was very ashamed to be exposed in front of everyone, caught by a trap set by his own son. He struggled to get free from the gum statue, which was melting in the sun.

As soon as he was able to move, he ran towards the trees on the other side of the farm. As he ran, the sticky gum, still clinging to his hands and feet, stretched to form long, silky threads behind him.

Those threads are still following Ananse today – they are called spider webs.

# How to catch a Niho

One evening in Aboakrom, just before the end of the great drought, there arrived a notorious hunting grasshopper from Wurakrom, a grassy plain next to Aboakrom. His name was Abebe, and he appeared on the main path of the forest, with a town crier.

They announced that, because of the drought, Abebe had been given permission by Nana Oppong to hunt  in the dense forest at the edge of the land of giants, a place called

the Giant Forest. Since the food was to be for the residents of both Wurakrom and Aboakrom, Abebe had to find a partner from Aboakrom to hunt with him.

"Which fool from Aboakrom is willing to join me? Which fool dares to hunt with Abebe?" the town crier roared.

Abebe followed the town crier, dancing and scraping his cutlass on the ground to make sparks.

Now, Abebe was known to be a skilled hunter, but he was also a cheat. Many people who had worked with him before had returned home empty-handed, so after a week of making the announcements, nobody from Aboakrom had volunteered to join the grasshopper.

Nevertheless, food was scarce and the residents of Aboakrom needed the meat from the hunt. They had all but given up when, one afternoon, Ananse came to the forest path and accepted Abebe's challenge.

Ananse had been hiding away since he got caught by the trap set by his own son. He had stayed in the forest to think, only going home once a week to see Aso Yaa. He realised that he had become very proud and unpleasant, and he had decided to change.

He walked up to Abebe. "I am your fool," he said. "When do we start?"

Abebe was very happy to see Ananse come to take the challenge. He had heard that the spider was not as clever as he used to be. It would be easy to cheat him. "Let's go now," he said.

☀ ☀ ☀

So Ananse and Abebe went deep into the Giant Forest.

As they got deeper they began to see many animal tracks. Ananse noticed that Abebe was excited, but Ananse pretended not to notice the tracks.

"Do you see what I see?" Abebe asked. 'We should be able to catch enough for your people and my people."

Ananse nodded.

Nana Oppong had ordered that they were not allowed to use bows and arrows. They could only set traps and could only set them once in each part of the Giant Forest.

They were supposed to share whatever they caught and take the spoils back to share with everyone in their part of the land. But Ananse noticed that Abebe had two traps to Ananse's one so that he would catch more food. He was a tricky little fellow, that Abebe!

At home, Aso Yaa and Ntikuma were shocked when Ananse told them about Abebe's traps.

"Are you just going to let him cheat you, Father?" asked Ntikuma.

"Oh, no," said Ananse, "I will let him cheat himself. Just wait and see."

☼ ☼ ☼

The next morning, Abebe was at Ananse's door before the sun could even blink.

"Ananse," he cried, "time to be a man and check those traps!"

Ananse ran out and set off for the Giant Forest with Abebe.

When they got to the traps they had set, only Ananse's trap had caught an animal. It was a grasscutter.

Ananse immediately volunteered to give the catch to Abebe. "My little friend, this is just a tiny rat so there is no need to share – you can have it. It is not the animal I want to catch."

Abebe was surprised that Ananse was prepared to share the catch from his trap, but he was sure there was a trick involved. "No, Ananse, I couldn't possibly take the catch from your trap."

"It's OK," said Ananse, "we can share the catch from the traps. The animal I want will take more than one trap. You take this and when we catch the big one, I'll take it."

"No, I insist," said Abebe, suddenly interested in Ananse's big catch. "You take this one and I'll take tomorrow's catch. I'm sure it will be bigger anyway."

"Are you sure?" said Ananse.

"Of course!" said Abebe.

They moved their traps further into the Giant Forest and Ananse went back to Aboakrom with the catch.

As soon as he arrived, Ntikuma ran to him. "What did you trap?"

"A huge grasscutter," said Ananse. "Call your mother and let's cook a pot of soup for everyone."

Within an hour, the residents of Aboakrom were sitting beneath the big mango tree beside the anthill eating the tastiest, spiciest soup they had had for a long, long time.

Ananse was everyone's idol again.

The next morning Ananse was waiting for Abebe on the path to the Giant Forest.

"Good morning, my friend," he said.

"Morning," Abebe grunted. "I hope today's catch is better. Everyone is blaming me because they had no meat yesterday."

"Don't worry. You will be a hero when you take the big catch home," said Ananse.

When they got to the traps, there was a wild hog caught in one of Abebe's traps.

"Ah, look!" exclaimed Ananse. "It's your good fortune. A tiny animal to take back with you. Tomorrow will be my turn and maybe I will get an antelope or that creature – a Niho."

Abebe glared at Ananse. "Look, don't think you can trick me. You take this hog back with you. Tomorrow I will take the antelope or that other creature you mentioned. I prefer antelope soup anyway."

So Ananse returned to Aboakrom with a wild hog and – again – everyone had a feast under the mango tree close to where Adanko, Ananse's old friend, lived.

Abebe, meanwhile, went back to Wurakrom with nothing.

The same thing happened the next day when Abebe and Ananse caught a duiker, and the day after, when they caught a forest hen.

Eventually, they caught an antelope.

Again, Ananse offered the antelope to Abebe,

saying that he only wanted to catch a creature called Niho that lived deeper in the forest in a place called Jemokokrom. What Abebe didn't know was that Jemokokrom simply meant no man's land – Ananse had made it up.

Of course Abebe, in his greed, refused the antelope. "Now that you have had all the little animals, the only thing that would make up for it is to catch that giant creature, Niho. You take the antelope. I will wait until we set the traps in Jemokokrom."

After ten days, Ananse and Abebe had set traps in almost every part of the Giant Forest and when they tried to move the traps further they came to a large bamboo fence.

"What is this?" asked Abebe.

"It's the end of the forest," laughed Ananse. "We can't hunt any more."

"But, but… but you told me that I could catch the Niho in Jemokokrom," protested Abebe.

Ananse pointed beyond the fence. "It's there, just before the land of the giants, but I can't go there with you. It is forbidden."

The grasshopper started crying. "Ananse, you tricked me. What will I say when I go home?"

"Tell them the truth," said Ananse. "Tell them that you tried to trick Ananse and you got tricked."

"Oh," cried Abebe, "I should have shared."

Ananse felt sorry for the little grasshopper

and held out his sack. "Abebe, you can share the porcupine that we caught today."

Abebe shook his head. "I told everyone that I was tricking you and I would bring back the biggest beast in the world. I will wait here until I catch something big."

The grasshopper continued to sob.

So Ananse had to leave Abebe the grasshopper crying in the Giant Forest and nobody has seen him hunting since then. However, if you happen to be in the forest or if you are very quiet at night you just might hear him crying.

This is how Ananse became a hero in Aboakrom again. He returned with a fine catch of porcupine and arrived just before evening, with the sun winking behind him. That night, everyone in Aboakrom feasted on porcupine stew and sang Ananse's praises. The mean tricks that he had played before were all forgotten.

⚙ ⚙ ⚙

But if you're travelling somewhere and you hear someone say 'no man's land', or if you meet a giant beast called Niho, think of Ananse the spider, the trickster of Aboakrom.

KP Kojo is the pen name of Nii Ayikwei Parkes, an award-winning novelist and poet. In 2010 he was shortlisted for the Commonwealth Writers' Prize for his adult novel *Tail of the Blue Bird* and the Michael Marks Award for his poetry pamphlet *ballast: a remix*. Raised in Ghana in Cape Coast and Accra, with short periods of residence in Kumasi and Tamale, KP Kojo grew up hearing stories from many different people – his father, his mother, his blind grandmother, orange sellers, watchmen, labourers, aunts, uncles, teachers, and a rag bag of friends with whom he ran wild in the dusty streets playing football and trading jokes and taunts. He never thought of becoming a storyteller for children himself until one afternoon in London he got a phone call asking him if he could visit a library and tell stories. Two days later he was kneeling in front of twenty six-year-olds retelling an Ananse story and making up new stories based on morals that the children had invented. That was in 2001. Since then he has worked in over 100 schools within the UK, using his moral-based storytelling techniques to teach pupils how to make up their own stories. *The Parade* is his first children's book.